The Super Special, Altogether Ordinary Day

Written by Kristen Heaney • Illustrated by Michael Molinet

The Super Special, Altogether Ordinary Day
Published by Blue Tide Press
Vero Beach, FL

ISBN: 978-0-9987537-1-3

JUVENILE FICTION / Family / Multigenerational

Designed and Illustrated by Michael Molinet

QUANTITY PURCHASES: Schools, companies, professional groups, clubs, and other organizations may qualify for special terms when ordering quantities of this title. For information, email Coach@InThreeGenerations.com

BLUE TIDE
PRESS

"Most days are ordinary days-
Most moments, ordinary moments.
The secret to leaving a lasting legacy
is to honor the extraordinary meaning in ordinary
moments spent with the ones you love."

~Kristen Heaney

In an altogether ordinary home...

...a bouncing boy raced down the stairs as fast as his feet could take him.

"Look! Do you see it?" said the grandmother.

"See what? Where?" said the little boy.

"A snake... slithering into the woods. It's black, and shiny, and very fast," said the grandmother.

"I do see it!" he hollered, running toward the snake.

But his Grandma knew he couldn't catch it.

It was a Black Racer, the swiftest and most skittish snake in the woods.

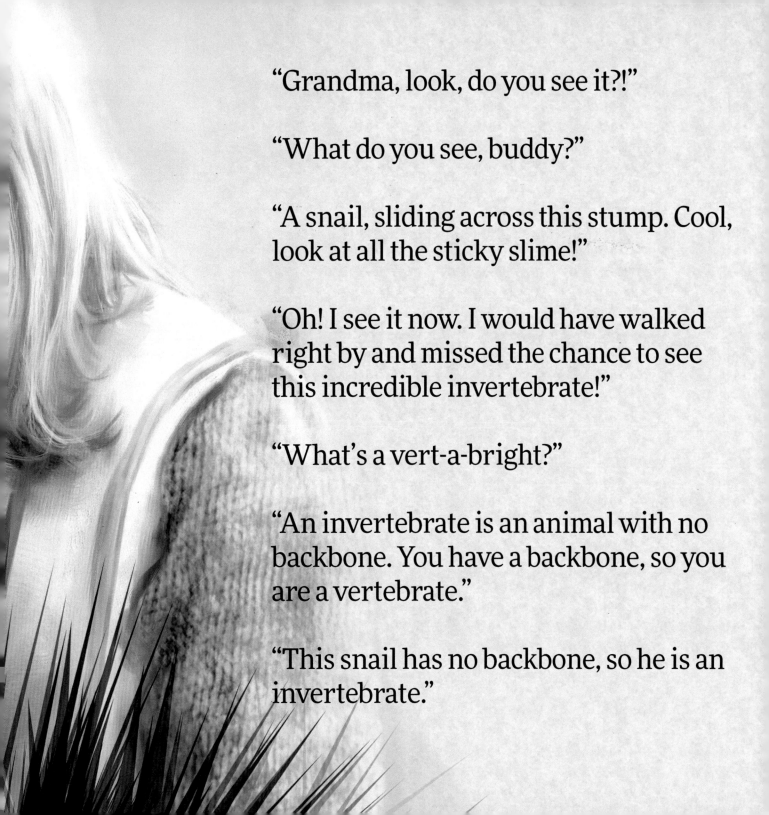

"Grandma, look, do you see it?!"

"What do you see, buddy?"

"A snail, sliding across this stump. Cool, look at all the sticky slime!"

"Oh! I see it now. I would have walked right by and missed the chance to see this incredible invertebrate!"

"What's a vert-a-bright?"

"An invertebrate is an animal with no backbone. You have a backbone, so you are a vertebrate."

"This snail has no backbone, so he is an invertebrate."

"Look!" they both exclaimed, pointing to a majestic Live Oak tree.
"It's the perfect climbing tree!" said the boy.
"It's the perfect shade tree!" said his grandmother.

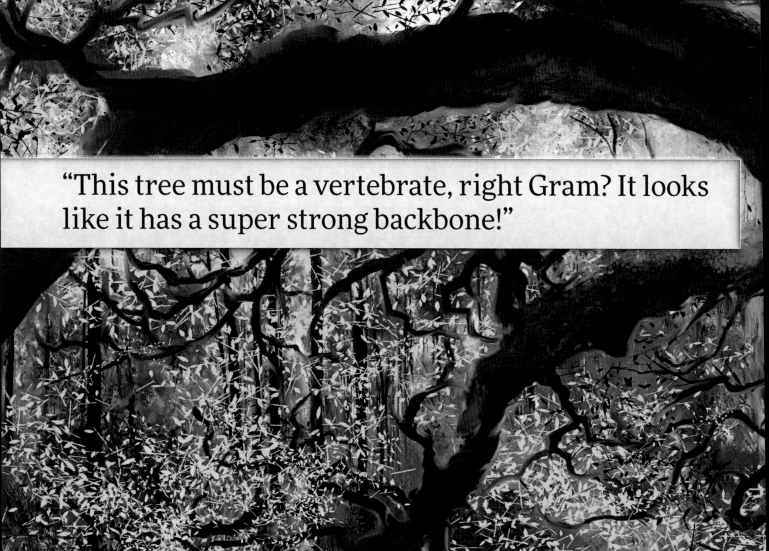

"This tree must be a vertebrate, right Gram? It looks like it has a super strong backbone!"

"Actually, it's not a vertebrate, but it's not an invertebrate, either! It's a plant, and we have different ways to classify plants. You're right about one thing - it is a very strong tree, and in that way it reminds me of a family tree."

"What's a family tree, Gram?"

"Some people say every family is like a tree. Look at the branches on this tree. Each one is unique, just like each person in our family."

The boy looked down and replied with a smile, "Except you and me."

"We're the same because Daddy says that we both have eyes that look like the starry sky."

"Yes, I was so happy when I first saw those bright blue eyes beaming back at me."

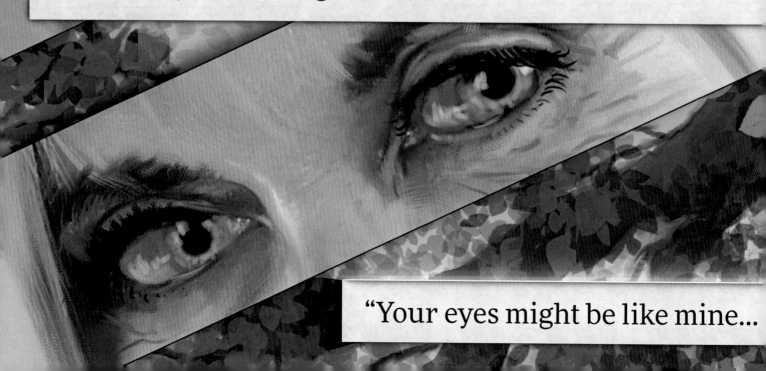

"Your eyes might be like mine...

...but you have endless energy just like your daddy did when he was your age."

"What about Annabelle? Is she a part of our family tree since she came to us from China instead of from Mom's belly?"

"Annabelle is just like this flower growing right into the tree branch. It's a part of the tree now."

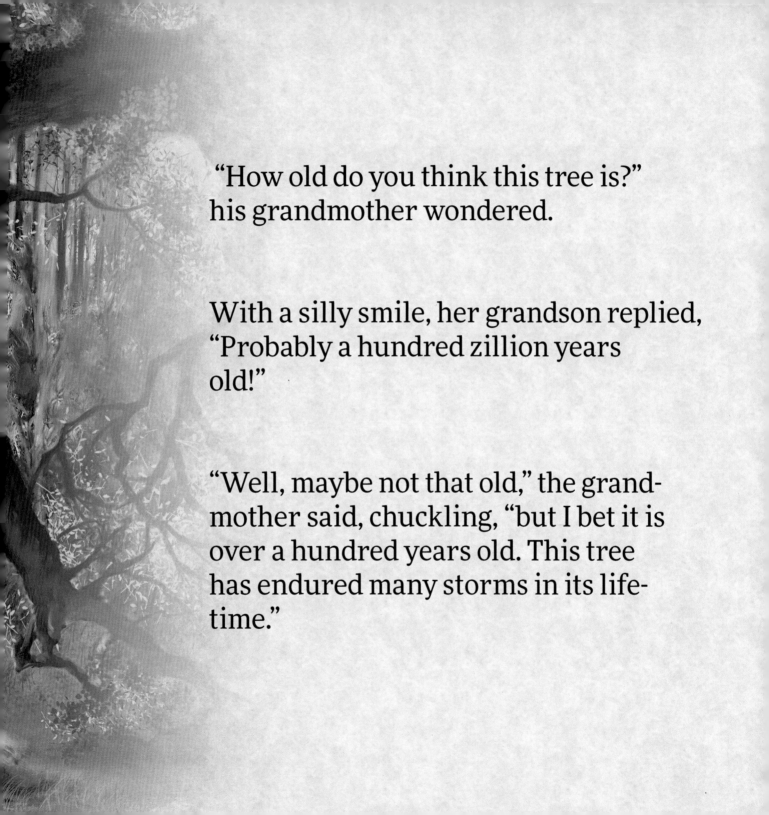

"How old do you think this tree is?" his grandmother wondered.

With a silly smile, her grandson replied, "Probably a hundred zillion years old!"

"Well, maybe not that old," the grandmother said, chuckling, "but I bet it is over a hundred years old. This tree has endured many storms in its lifetime."

"You're right. This tree and our own family tree made it through that storm because we have very strong roots."

"Do you mean our prayers? And the kind things we do? And our memories of playing games and eating yummy pies at your house every Thanksgiving?" he asked.

"That's exactly right, my brilliant boy," his Grandmother smiled.

"Hey, Gram, can we go home and draw a picture of our family tree?" the boy asked with hope in his eyes.

"What a great idea! I've got construction paper and markers at the house."

"Markers? Mom likes for me to stick with crayons because she says I get too messy with the markers."

"Too messy?"

"Yeah, Mom and Dad didn't think the welcome home message I drew all over Annabelle's bedroom walls looked as cool as I thought it did. So now I have to get special permission before I can touch the markers."

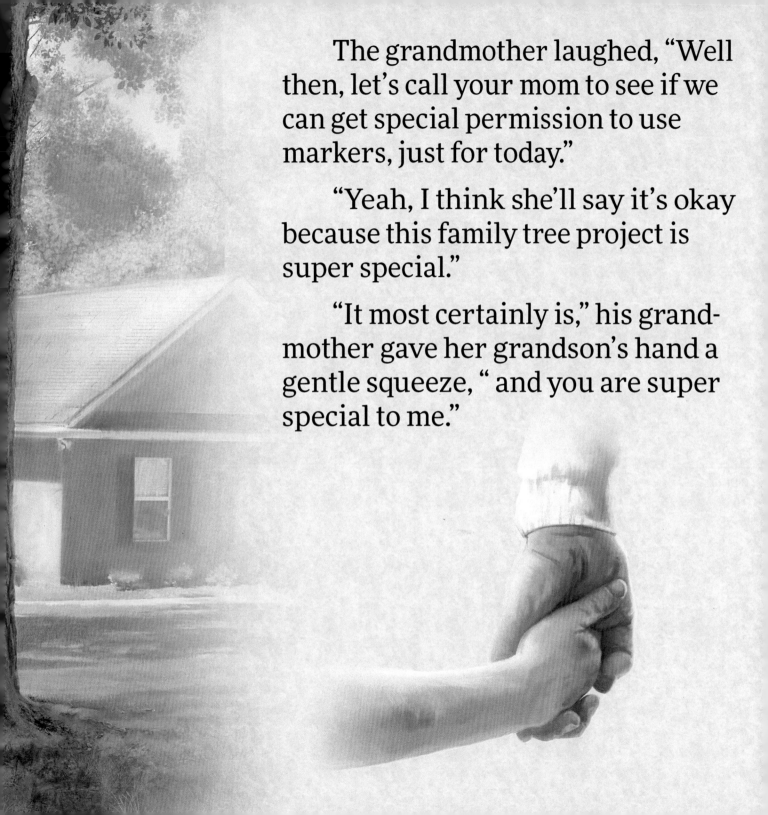

The grandmother laughed, "Well then, let's call your mom to see if we can get special permission to use markers, just for today."

"Yeah, I think she'll say it's okay because this family tree project is super special."

"It most certainly is," his grand-mother gave her grandson's hand a gentle squeeze, " and you are super special to me."

Want to enjoy some fun activities inspired by this book?

Visit **www.inthreegenerations.com/SuperSpecial**

- **Alliteration Hunt** - Learn about alliteration, and then hunt for alliteration hidden throughout this book.

- **Family Tree Project -** Use this page to get you started in making your own family tree together.

- **Nature Walk Scavenger Hunt -** Take this printable page with you on a nature walk, and see how many items you can find together!

Additional Resources for Grandparents

Learn more about my work helping families share legacy values across generations
www.legacycapitals.com

Check out my first book, *In Three Generations: A Story about Family, Wealth, and Beating the Odds* at **www.inthreegenerations.com**

Connect with me
www.linkedin.com/in/legacyconsultant

Email me
coach@in3generations.com

Meet the Author

In her work as a Wealth Legacy Coach, Kristen Heaney helps successful families connect across generations at the intersection of values, purpose, and financial success. Her passion for this work is colored by her own experience of being a young and unprepared inheritor after her father's early death. Kristen's training includes a Masters in Social Work from the University of Michigan, a Board Certified Coaching credential, and an advanced certificate in Family Wealth Advising from the Family Firm Institute.

Her debut book, In Three Generations: A Story About Family, Wealth, and Beating the Odd is a heartfelt family parable, offering a great starting point for those considering a more purposeful approach to handling family wealth across generations. She has been a featured thought leader for the Purposeful Planning Institute, Aspiriant's MoneyTale$ and I'm a Millionnaire! So Now What? podcasts, as well as legal, financial, and philanthropic firms across the United States and Canada, discussing topics such as rising generation preparation, effective family meetings, wealthism, entitlement, and financial parenting. Kristen was born and raised in the Metro Detroit area, and currently lives with her husband and two sons in South Florida.

Meet the Illustrator

From boyhood, author/illustrator Michael Molinet has used imagination and an idiomatic perspective to understand and live in the world around him. Ever encouraging others to think their own thoughts and to live out their own story honestly, he shares his own though the medium of art, writing and his own publications. Believing that all people are precious, loved and given purpose, he hopes that through their narrative they find, choose, and become the best version of themselves.

Mike lives in Colorado with his wife Andi and his children, each in their own stage of discovery within their own stories, of which he is privileged to be a part.

Made in United States
North Haven, CT
22 July 2022

21700211R00024